Woody Needs a home

BY VELMA LACCETTI

To order additional copies of this title, contact your favorite local bookstore or visit www.tbmbooks.com.

Cover and book design by Stacey Leonard.

Printed in the United States of America.

The Troy Book Makers
www.thetroybookmakers.com

ISBN: 978-1-61468-363-6

Woody

Needs a home

BY VELMA LACCETTI

THIS BOOK IS DEDICATED TO MY CHILDREN AND GRANDCHILDREN WHO INSPIRED ME
WITH THEIR KINDNESS AND CARING FOR OTHER PEOPLE.

THIS BOOK IS ALSO DEDICATED TO ALL THE CHILDREN OUT THERE
WHO CHOOSE TO BE KIND AND COMPASSIONATE.

AND TO THOSE OF YOU, YOUNG OR OLD, WHO GO OUT OF YOUR WAY TO BE A FRIEND
TO ALL WHO NEED ONE, NO MATTER ONE'S OUTWARD APPEARANCE, I WISH YOU THE
HAPPIEST OF LIVES. YOU TRULY ARE MAKING A DIFFERENCE IN THE WORLD.

SO WOODY SET OFF ON AN ADVENTURE TO FIND A NEW HOME AND NEW FRIENDS WHO WOULD ACCEPT HIM JUST THE WAY HE WAS.

AFTER A DAY OR TWO OF SEARCHING, WOODY WAS SO HAPPY TO DISCOVER A TREE FULL OF PLUMP, JUICY PEARS.

HE BECAME **EVEN MORE** EXCITED **WHEN** HE SAW PORCH STAIRS **UNDER** WHICH HE **COULD LIVE, RIGHT** BY THE PEAR **TREE!**

BUT WHAT WOODY DIDN'T SEE WERE SIGNS STATING THAT THIS WAS FARMER JOHN'S PORCH, AND THAT WAS FARMER JOHN'S PEAR TREE, AND ABSOLUTELY NO WOODCHUCKS WERE ALLOWED.

ABSOLUTELY NO WOODCHUCKS ALLOWED!!!!!

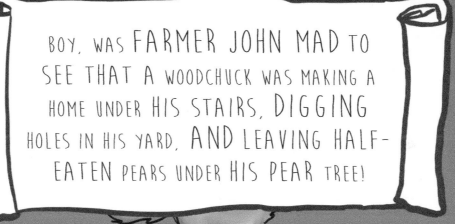

SO, WHILE WOODY WAS SETTLING IN, FARMER JOHN BEGAN PLOTTING WAYS TO SCARE WOODY OFF HIS PROPERTY.

MAYBE, ONCE THE ANGRY FARMER SEES HOW NICELY MY HOUSE IS COMING ALONG, HE WILL LEAVE ME ALONE!

HE SET TRAPS... BUT WOODY WAS TOO SMART. FARMER JOHN YELLED AND SCREAMED... BUT WOODY HAS LITTLE EARS AND BARELY HEARD HIM.

I BET HE LIKES BONES. ALL DOGS LOVE BONES! THEN HE WILL DEFINITELY WANT TO BE MY FRIEND! MUST-FIND-BONES!

HE DECIDED THE ONLY WAY HE COULD DO THAT WOULD BE BY TALKING TO FRED.

I BET HE LIKES PEARS. ALL WOODCHUCKS LOVE PEARS! THAT WILL BE THE TRICK TO CATCHING THIS RASCAL! MUST-FIND-PEARS!

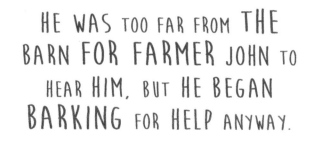

HE WAS TOO FAR FROM THE BARN FOR FARMER JOHN TO HEAR HIM, BUT HE BEGAN BARKING FOR HELP ANYWAY.

RUFF! RUFF!
RUFF, RUFF, RUFF!

NO MATTER HOW OTHERS TREAT YOU, YOU MUST ALWAYS TREAT OTHERS THE WAY YOU WANT TO BE TREATED!

WOODY HAS A GOOD HEART, AND WAS EXCITED TO SHOW FRED AND FARMER JOHN THAT HE WOULD MAKE A GREAT FRIEND IF THEY ONLY GAVE HIM A CHANCE.

WOODY, PLEASE FIND FARMER JOHN! IT'S GOING TO BE DARK SOON! HURRY!

WOODY SOON FOUND FRED ALONG THE PATH, AND ALTHOUGH HE TRIED WITH ALL HIS MIGHT, HE COULDN'T SET FRED FREE.

SO WOODY **RAN** AS **FAST** AS **HE COULD** UNTIL **HE** REACHED **FARMER JOHN,** AND LED FARMER JOHN **BACK** TO **WHERE FRED** WAS STUCK.

FRED WAS FINALLY SET FREE. HE AND FARMER JOHN COULDN'T BELIEVE HOW HELPFUL AND FRIENDLY WOODY CHOSE TO BE AFTER THEY HAD TREATED HIM SO POORLY. SO FARMER JOHN AND FRED THANKED WOODY, AND APOLOGIZED FOR BEING MEAN TO HIM.

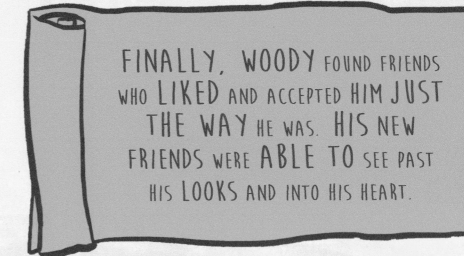

FINALLY, WOODY FOUND FRIENDS WHO LIKED AND ACCEPTED HIM JUST THE WAY HE WAS. HIS NEW FRIENDS WERE ABLE TO SEE PAST HIS LOOKS AND INTO HIS HEART.

KIND WAYS ARE ALWAYS THE BEST WAYS.

WOODY WAS **HAPPY**, FRED WAS **HAPPY**, AND **FARMER JOHN** WAS HAPPY, **TOO!**